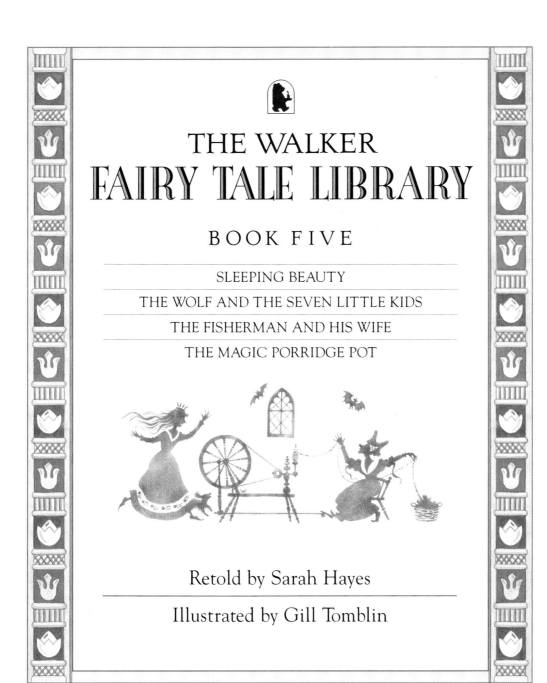

THE WALKER
FAIRY TALE LIBRARY

BOOK FIVE

Retold by Sarah Hayes

Illustrated by Gill Tomblin

SLEEPING BEAUTY

Once upon a time there lived a king and queen who were very unhappy because they had no children. After many years, when they had almost given up hope, the queen gave birth to a beautiful daughter.

A grand christening was arranged, and seven fairies were asked to be godmothers to the baby princess. At the magnificent christening feast seven places of honour were laid for the seven godmothers. In front of each fairy stood a gold goblet studded with rubies and diamonds and a gold knife, fork and spoon.

As the guests sat down to dinner, a mumbling and a muttering was heard outside the hall. In hobbled an ancient fairy, in a temper as black as thunder.

She lived in a high tower in the castle and had not been seen for fifty years. The king, the queen and everyone in the castle had forgotten all about her.

A place was hastily laid, but there was no gold goblet or knife, fork and spoon for the aged fairy, and she had to make do with silver. She sat down muttering words of revenge under her breath. A young fairy who was sitting nearby heard these threats and feared for the princess's safety. So while the other godmothers gathered to present their gifts, the young fairy crept behind the curtains.

One by one the fairies gave their gifts to the princess. The youngest gave the gift of beauty; the next gave good nature; the third the gift of grace; the fourth the art of dancing; the fifth said the princess would sing like a nightingale; and the sixth that she would be able to play any musical instrument she chose.

Then, shaking with fury, the aged fairy stood up and pointed a bony finger at the baby in the

cradle. 'My gift to the princess is this,' she said.
'When she reaches her sixteenth birthday, the
princess will prick her finger on a spindle and die!'
A gasp of horror ran round the court. Then the
young fairy stepped out from behind the curtains.

'I have not the power to undo this evil spell,' said she, 'but my gift to the princess is this: when she reaches her sixteenth birthday, she will indeed prick her finger, but she will not die. Instead she will go to sleep for a hundred years, and then a prince will come and wake her.'

The princess grew up to be as beautiful as the fairies had wished. The king banned all spindles and spinning wheels throughout the land, and the wicked fairy's spell was quite forgotten until the day of the princess's sixteenth birthday.

The princess was wandering through the castle when she discovered a little winding staircase she had not seen before. At the top of the stairs she found a room where an old woman sat spinning. The woman had never heard the proclamation banning spinning wheels.

The princess watched the spindle spin round and listened to the whirr of the wheel. 'Oh, please may I try?' she asked, but no sooner had she taken hold of the thread than the spindle pricked her finger and she fell to the ground.

Horrified, the old woman called for help. People came running but none could revive the princess, who lay fast asleep, a slight smile on her lips. The king ordered a great bed to be made, hung with tapestries embroidered in gold and silver. The young fairy was summoned, but there was nothing she could do. When she saw the sleeping princess lying on her great gold and silver bed, she was concerned. 'How frightened the princess will be,' she said to herself, 'when she wakes up in a hundred years and finds herself alone and everything changed.' So the fairy made sure that nothing *would* change. She went from room to room touching everyone and everything with her wand. Ladies dressing, gentlemen drinking, soldiers on guard, cooks rolling pastry, boys turning spits, cats about to pounce, horses kicking stable doors – all fell into a deep sleep at a touch of the wand. Even the princess's little spaniel lay snoring at the foot of the gold and silver bed.

Years passed and a great forest of tangled

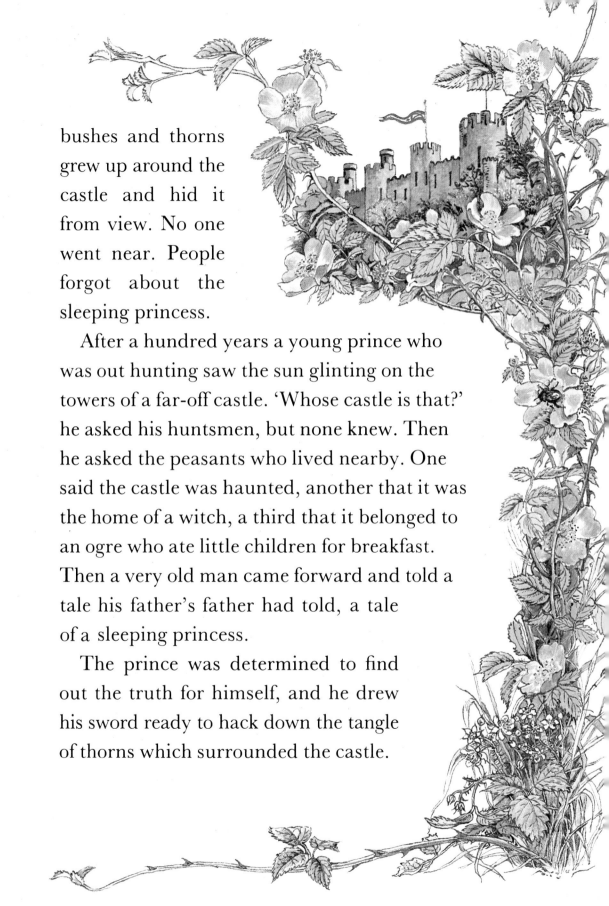

bushes and thorns grew up around the castle and hid it from view. No one went near. People forgot about the sleeping princess.

After a hundred years a young prince who was out hunting saw the sun glinting on the towers of a far-off castle. 'Whose castle is that?' he asked his huntsmen, but none knew. Then he asked the peasants who lived nearby. One said the castle was haunted, another that it was the home of a witch, a third that it belonged to an ogre who ate little children for breakfast. Then a very old man came forward and told a tale his father's father had told, a tale of a sleeping princess.

The prince was determined to find out the truth for himself, and he drew his sword ready to hack down the tangle of thorns which surrounded the castle.

But miraculously the branches drew back at his approach and the thorns turned aside, only to close in again as he passed, so that no one could follow. The prince walked on through the hedge of briars until he reached a vast courtyard filled with people so still he thought they were dead, but then he saw they were breathing.

On went the prince through the castle and up the stairs to the room with the gold and silver bed. There he saw the princess, and as he knelt down to kiss her, she opened her eyes and said, 'At last my prince has come. How long you have kept me waiting!'

The prince was so overcome he didn't know what to say. But the princess could hardly stop talking, and while she talked people all over the castle began to wake up and go about their business. The prince and princess were married that very day and lived happily ever after.

THE WOLF AND
THE SEVEN LITTLE KIDS

Deep in the forest lived a mother goat and her
seven little kids. One day the mother goat had
to go out for food.

'You must take great care, my dears,' she said
to the seven little kids. 'There is a wicked wolf
in the forest, and you must not let him in, or he
will eat you up. You will know him by his rough
voice and his black paws.'

'Do not worry, Mother. We will take great
care,' said the oldest kid, and the mother goat
set off. She had not gone far before the wolf
crept up to the door.

'Open the door, children dear,' he said in a
rough voice. 'Here is your mother come home
with a present for each of you.'

'We will not open the door!' shouted the kids.

'We know from your voice you are not our mother. You are the wolf!' The wolf went off and gulped down a huge lump of chalk to make his voice smooth. He crept up to the door again.

'Open the door, children dear,' he said in a voice as smooth as butter. 'Here is your mother come home with a present for each of you.' But the kids saw his black paws resting on the window.

'We will not open the door!' shouted the kids. 'We know from your paws you are not our mother. You are the wolf!'

The wolf went off and found a baker. 'Give me some dough,

Baker, to put on my hurt paw.' The baker gave him some dough, and the wolf spread the dough on both his paws. Then he found a miller. 'Flour my paws, Miller, or I'll eat you up,' he said.

The miller suspected the wolf was up to no good, but what could he do? So he dusted the wolf's paws with flour and let him go.

Again the wolf crept up to the little kids' door. 'Open the door, children dear. Here is your mother come home with a present for each of you.' The kids heard the voice as smooth as butter, saw the paws as white as milk, and they opened the door.

In rushed the wolf.

Round and round ran the kids, trying to hide. One hid under the table, one in the bed, one in the oven, one in the larder, one in the cupboard and one in the washing bowl. The youngest of all climbed into the grandfather clock. The wolf soon found them and ate them up – all, that is, except for the littlest kid, who shivered and shook in the clock.

When the mother goat returned, what a sight met her eyes! The door was wide open, the table turned over, the bed-clothes rumpled, the larder and cupboard in a mess, the washing bowl upset. She called her children, but no one answered until the littlest kid bleated out from the grandfather clock, 'Here I am, Mother!' and told her what had happened.

The mother goat rushed into the forest, weeping for her lost children.

Not far from the house she found the wolf lying on the grass, fast asleep after his feast. 'Quick,' she said to the littlest kid. 'Run home and fetch scissors, thread and needle.' She had seen something moving inside the wolf's stomach.

When the littlest kid returned, the mother goat took the scissors and carefully snipped open the wolf's stomach. Out hopped one, two, three, four, five, six little kids. 'Quick,' the mother goat said to the kids. 'Each of you run off and fetch a big stone.' When they returned, she put the stones into the wolf's stomach and neatly stitched it up again.

When the wolf woke up, he felt very uncomfortable with all the stones rattling about inside him. He was very thirsty and went to find a well, moaning:

'What rumbles and tumbles
Inside my poor bones?
It should be six kids
But feels like six stones.'

He leant over the well to drink, but the stones were so heavy that he fell in and was drowned. The kids all joined hands and skipped round the well singing, 'The wolf is dead! The wolf is dead! The wicked wolf is dead!'

THE FISHERMAN
AND HIS WIFE

There was once a poor fisherman who lived
with his wife in a tumbledown shack by the sea.
Every day he would go to the seashore and
catch fish for supper. One day his fishing line
was drawn down, down, into the depths of the
cool green water. The fisherman pulled and
pulled and up came a flounder.

To his astonishment the flounder began to
speak. 'Listen to me, Fisherman. I am not really
a fish, but an enchanted prince. Do not eat me.
Throw me back and let me swim away.'

'I could never eat a talking fish,' said the
fisherman, and he threw the flounder back.
When he got home and told his wife the story,
she scowled.

'Didn't you ask for anything in return?'

'No, Wife. We need nothing for ourselves.'

'Nothing!' shrieked the wife. 'Here we are living in this tumbledown shack, and you ask for nothing! Go back to that fish and ask for a cottage.'

So the fisherman went back to the seashore and called:

> 'Flounder, flounder in the sea,
> Or prince, if prince you rightly be.
> Such a greedy wife I've got,
> She wants something I do not.'

The sea grew blue and oily. The flounder swam up to the surface. 'Well, what is it she wants?'

'A cottage, Sir,' said the fisherman, 'if that's all right.'

'Go home and you will find one,' said the fish, and he swam away.

The fisherman walked home, and there stood the sweetest cottage imaginable. Roses rambled round the door; a shiny stove was cooking supper in the little kitchen; a fine brass bed

stood in the upstairs bedroom; carrots and peas
grew in the back garden; and chickens and
goats wandered about the paddock. The
fisherman's wife was delighted.

By the end of the week she was scowling
again. 'This cottage is too small for us. Go and
ask that fish for a castle.'

'We don't need a castle,' said the fisherman.
'Anyway the fish may be angry.'

'If he can give us a cottage, he can give us a
castle. Go *now*!'

So the fisherman went back to the seashore
and called:

> '*Flounder, flounder in the sea,*
> *Or prince, if prince you rightly be.*
> *Such a greedy wife I've got,*
> *She wants something I do not.*'

The sea heaved and swelled, then turned grey
and smoky. The flounder swam to the surface.
'Well, what does she want now?'

'A castle, Sir, if you please,' said the
fisherman, trembling.

'Go home and you will find one.'

The fisherman walked back, and there in front
of him stood a huge castle with towers and turrets
and battlements. There were chandeliers and
tapestries, banqueting halls and ballrooms, wine
cellars and cupolas. Servants scurried everywhere.
The fisherman's wife was beside herself with joy.

After a few days she was scowling again. 'Look out of the window, Husband. What do you see?'

'A garden, a fountain, an orchard filled with fruit trees,' the fisherman replied.

'And beyond?'

'Beyond I see fields.'

'Not *our* fields, Husband. Go back to that fish and ask for those fields. Say I want to be queen.'

'The fish will be furious. Haven't we had enough?'

'If he can give us a castle, he can make me queen. Go NOW!'

So the fisherman went back to the seashore and called:

> *'Flounder, flounder in the sea,*
> *Or prince, if prince you rightly be.*
> *Such a greedy wife I've got,*
> *She wants something I do not.'*

The sea boiled. Huge waves crashed on the shore. The flounder swam up to the surface. 'Well, what is it?'

'She wants to be queen, Your Honour,' said the fisherman, terrified.

'Go home and you will find her queen,' said the fish, and he swam away. The fisherman walked back to the castle and saw flags flying and guards standing to attention at the gate. His wife was sitting on a gold and velvet throne, wearing an enormous crown that sparkled with jewels.

'There's *nothing* more she can want,' thought the fisherman. But he was wrong, for the very next day his wife was scowling again.

'Look out of the window, Husband. What do you see?'

'A garden and fields and all the lands around.'

'And beyond?'

'Beyond I see nothing but the sun shining and the sky.'

'Then that's what I want. Go and tell that fish I want to make the sun rise and the moon set.'

The fisherman was horrified. 'No one can have power over the sun and moon, Wife. You cannot ask the fish for that.'

The fisherman's wife stamped her foot. 'I can and I will! Go NOW!' So the fisherman walked slowly back to the seashore and called:

'Flounder, flounder in the sea,
Or prince, if prince you rightly be.
Such a greedy wife I've got,
She wants something I do not.'

The wind raged. Lightning flashed across the sky. The sea grew black and formed a whirlpool. The flounder swam up to the surface. 'Well?'

'Your Highness, she wants to make the sun rise and the moon set,' said the poor fisherman.

'Go home,' thundered the fish. 'Go home to your wife and your tumbledown shack.'

So the fisherman walked home and found his wife sitting in the tumbledown shack. And there they had to live for the rest of their days.

THE MAGIC PORRIDGE POT

There was once a poor girl who lived alone with her mother. One day the girl set off into the forest to gather berries. There she met an old woman who saw how poor and hungry she was.

'Take this pot,' the old woman said, handing the girl an ordinary brown cooking pot. 'Just lift the lid and say "Cook, little pot, cook." When you have eaten enough, just say "Stop, little pot, stop." You need never be hungry again.'

The girl thanked the old woman and took the pot home. She lifted the lid and said, 'Cook, little pot, cook.' Straight away the little pot started to heave and bubble and fill with delicious porridge. When the girl had eaten enough, she said, 'Stop, little pot, stop.' The little pot stopped, and she put back the lid.

Now the girl and her mother were hungry no more, and all went well until the day the mother wanted some porridge while her daughter was out. 'Cook, little pot, cook,' she said, lifting the lid of the little pot which started to heave and bubble and fill with porridge.

When she had eaten enough, the mother tried to stop the pot. But she did not know the right words. She tried to put the lid on, but the little pot went on cooking until the porridge rose over the edge. It cooked and it cooked until the whole house was filled with porridge, and then the next house, and the next, until the whole village was filled with porridge, all except for one house on the very edge of the village.

At that moment the girl came home. 'Stop, little pot, stop,' she said when she saw the porridge rolling up to the door of the last house. The porridge stopped heaving and bubbling, and the little pot stopped cooking. And from that day to this, anyone who wants to visit the village has to eat a path through the porridge.